THE THREE L|||ES

and the Big

Roger Hargreaves

Original concept by
Roger Hargreaves

Written and illustrated by
Adam Hargreaves

EGMONT

Little Miss Naughty had decided to build a new house for herself. But because she did not know how to build a house, she asked her good friend Mr Silly to build it for her.

And he did.

He made it with straw.

A house built of straw?

How silly!

But it was not just silly, it was also dangerous because not long after Little Miss Naughty had moved in, the Big Bad Wolf came calling.

He knocked on Little Miss Naughty's straw door.

"Little Miss," called the wolf. "It's the Big Bad Wolf. Won't you let me come in?"

"Not on your Nellie," replied Little Miss Naughty, cheekily. "I won't let you in."

"Then I'll huff and I'll puff and I'll blow your house down," cried the wolf.

And he did, because that is the sort of thing that Big Bad Wolves get up to.

But Little Miss Naughty had had a lot of practice at jumping out of windows, the naughty girl!

She leaped out of the back window and ran all the way through the woods to the house of her friend, Little Miss Trouble.

Now, as it so happened, Little Miss Trouble had also just had a house built for herself.

A house built by Mr Mean.

And as you probably know Mr Mean does not like to spend money, so he had built Little Miss Trouble's house as cheaply as he could.

He had built it with sticks.

A house built of sticks?

How mean!

Shortly after Little Miss Naughty arrived, the wolf, who had followed her, knocked on the door.

"Little Miss and Little Miss, it's the Big Bad Wolf. Won't you let me come in?"

"Not on your Nellie! We will not let you in!" they replied.

"Then I'll huff and I'll puff and I'll blow your house down!" cried the wolf.

And he did.

So the two Little Misses ran out of the back door and stole Mr Funny's car.

I know! How naughty!

They raced off to Little Miss Bad's house with the wolf chasing after them.

Little Miss Bad had employed a proper builder to build her house.

Mr Brick.

Brick by name and brick by nature.

So, of course, he had made Little Miss Bad's house out of bricks.

Not long after the two Little Misses burst into Little Miss Bad's house, there was a knock at the door.

"That will be the Big Bad Wolf," said Little Miss Naughty.

"This is the Big Bad Wolf …" began the wolf.

"We know!" chorused the three Little Misses.

"Little Miss, Little Miss and Little Miss, won't you let me come in?" asked the wolf.

"Not on your Nellie! We won't let you come in!" cried the three Little Misses.

"Then I'll huff and I'll puff and I'll blow your house down!" roared the wolf.

And he did.

Or, at least he huffed and puffed, but Little Miss Bad's brick house did not fall down.

It was too strong.

"Bother," said the wolf.

And then he had another idea.

"Little Miss, Little Miss and Little Miss, I know of a lovely orchard on a hill on Mr Field's farm. Will you meet me there tomorrow morning at seven o'clock? We can have apples for breakfast?"

The three Little Misses agreed.

They had a plan.

The three Little Misses were not just naughty, trouble and bad, they were also clever. The next day, they got up at six o'clock to get to the orchard ahead of the Wolf and set a trap for him.

But the Wolf, who was even more clever, had arrived even earlier.

"Got you!" he cried, leaping out from his hiding place behind an apple tree.

At first, the three Little Misses were frightened.

And then Little Miss Naughty had a thought.

For the first time in their lives they could be naughty, troublesome and bad and they would be in the right!

"You might be Big and you might be Bad," said Little Miss Naughty, "but I am Naughty."

"And I am Trouble," said Little Miss Trouble.

"And I am Bad!" said Little Miss Bad.

"And we'll huff and we'll puff and we'll blow *you* down!" cried the three Little Misses all together.

And they did.

They huffed and they puffed and they blew the
Big Bad Wolf all the way down the hill.

The Wolf rolled and bounced and bumped so much
you might *almost* have felt sorry for him.

But not quite.